The Story of
Thumbelina

Illustrated by Suzy-Jane Tanner

It's fun to Read Along

Here's what you do-

These pictures are some of the characters and things the story tells about. Let the child to whom you are reading SEE and SAY them.

Then, as you read the story text and come to a picture instead of a word, pause and point to the picture for your listener to SEE and SAY.

You'll be amazed at how quickly children catch on and enjoy participating in the story telling.

ISBN 0-86163-812-3

Copyright © 1989 Award Publications Limited
This edition first published 1996
Sixth impression 2004

Published by Award Publications Limited,
27 Longford Street, London NW1 3DZ

Printed in Malaysia

apples

bird

birds

butterfly

clouds

cottage

fairies

dress

door

crown

fishes

leaf

river

Thumbelina

flower

Mr Mole

spiders

toad

flowers

Mrs Mouse

snow

walnut shell

Flower King

poor woman

sunshine

window

girl

pot

thumb

witch

Once upon a time a knocked on the of a little  where a good lived. The  gave her a gift of red and told the how she longed for a child.

The gave the a  and told her to plant it in a . The did this and it soon grew into a beautiful  . The kissed the  with

joy and as it opened wide the  saw a tiny .

The called the  because she was no bigger than her . All day long, danced and sang.

At night, she slept in a with a rose petal for a blanket.

One night, as  lay asleep, a fat  hopped in through broken glass in the . She thought  would make a pretty wife for her son.

The  carried the off
to her home on the riverbank.

Poor was left all alone on a big broad in the middle of the . The old and her son had gone to get ready for the wedding. was unhappy. She did not want to marry a .

The little heard her sobs. They felt sorry for pretty little , so they nibbled through the stem of the .

Set free, the  floated down the . Wild sang sweetly as she passed by. A pretty settled next to . She tied one end of her

sash to the  and the other to the . They floated on down the and pulled into a bank beside a meadow. lived happily amongst the summer .

Then winter came and  lay thick upon the ground.

Poor became very cold and hungry. At last, she came upon a . It was the home of , who took her into the warm parlour. said that could stay all winter. In return, must tidy the parlour and tell stories to to help pass away the long winter evenings. did all those things very well and was very pleased.

One day, rich , who lived at the end of a dark tunnel, came on a visit. could not see very well but when he heard sing he fell in love with her sweet voice. Next day, when and visited , he told them not to be bothered by a dead bird in the tunnel. did not like .

reminded too much of things he did not like, such as and bright .

This poor had fallen in through a hole in the roof of the tunnel.

That night, went back and gently covered the with thistledown. He was not dead and cared for him in secret until he was well enough to fly away.

"I shall miss you," told the .

One day, told that she must marry . She hired six to spin silk for new clothes. was put to work making her own wedding while was busy in the kitchen. Poor did not want to marry rich and live in the dark underground. She begged just once more to see the and the .

As stood in the her friend the flew down to her. "Come with me to the South," he said. "There, you will be happy in the ." climbed up onto his back.

Away they flew, far away from  and his dark home. At last they came to a lovely garden. The set down amongst the .

On one pretty [flower] sat the [king]. When he saw [princess] he put a [crown] upon her head and asked her to be his Queen. All the [fairy] came with gifts for [princess]. The best gift of all was a pair of silver wings, so [princess] could fly happily all day from  to [flower]. Later the [king] married [princess] and they lived happily ever after.